THE CROCODILE AND THE SCORPION

Copyright © 2013 by Rebecca Emberley Inc.
A Neal Porter Book
Published by Roaring Brook Press
Roaring Brook Press is a division of Holtzbrinck Publishing Holdings Limited Partnership
175 Fifth Avenue, New York, New York 10010
mackids.com

Library of Congress Cataloging-in-Publication Data

Emberley, Rebecca.
   The crocodile and the scorpion / Rebecca Emberley and Ed Emberley.—First edition.
      pages cm
   "A Neal Porter Book."
   Summary: "Based on the classic fable, a crocodile and a scorpion attempt to cross a
river without giving in to their natural instincts"—Provided by publisher.
   ISBN 978-1-59643-494-3 (hardcover : alk. paper)
   [1. Fables.]   I. Emberley, Ed.   II. Title.
   PZ8.2.E543Cro 2013
   398.2—dc23
   [E]

2012046933

Roaring Brook Press books are available for special promotions and premiums. For details
contact: Director of Special Markets, Holtzbrinck Publishers.

First edition 2013
Book design by Andrew Arnold

Printed in China by South China Printing Co. Ltd., Dongguan City, Guangdong Province

10 9 8 7 6 5 4 3 2 1

REBECCA EMBERLEY
and ED EMBERLEY

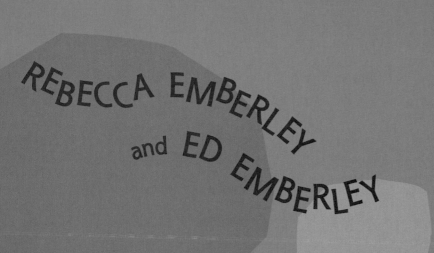

THE CROCODILE AND THE SCORPION

A Neal Porter Book

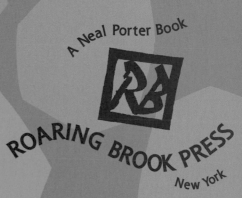

ROARING BROOK PRESS
New York

The crocodile lived on the banks of the great big, brilliant blue river. His appetite was very large. His brain was very small.

The scorpion lived not far away in some rocks. His stinger was very sharp, but his mind was not.

They both had brains no bigger than a pebble, which did not serve them very well, as you will see.

One morning, for reasons known only to him, the scorpion left the rocks and made his way to the great big, brilliant blue river.

He didn't know much, but he knew he couldn't cross the river on his own.

The crocodile was lying in the sun, thinking only of the next fish dinner he would eat.

The scorpion scuttled over to the crocodile.

"Excuse me" he said. "I would like to cross the river and it looks like I am going to need some help. Would you be so kind?" he asked.

The crocodile, slightly annoyed to be disturbed from his fishy thoughts, rumbled sleepily, "Have you no friends who can help you?"

"No, no friends. I don't have any friends because I am always stinging things and they seem not to like it," said the scorpion matter-of-factly.

The crocodile turned this over in his very small brain. "I, too, have no friends. I am always biting things and they seem not to like that, either."

"We could be friends," said the scorpion.

"Yes, we could," replied the crocodile.

Neither of them had the slightest idea of what this really meant.

"Then I could ride on your back across the river to the other side."

"You promise not to sting me?" asked the crocodile.

"If you promise not to bite me," countered the scorpion.

So the scorpion krickety-klacked onto the crocodile and they set out to cross the river.

The scorpion could not restrain himself.
Within moments he skittered about the
crocodiles back and stung him!

The crocodile opened his
jaws and

SNAP!

lunged at the scorpion.

"You promised not to bite!"

"THiS iS

ALL YOUR

they shouted as they sank
to the bottom of the great big,
brilliant blue river.

If you happen to find yourself at the edge of the great river and you put your ear to the water you can hear them arguing still . . . that is if someone has not settled the argument for them.